The Breaking Point

Applying Biblical Principle In Life Situation

Anterral Taylor

Copyright © 2021 Anterral Taylor
All Rights Reserved

Table of Contents

Chapter One
Face It Or Leave It..1

Chapter Two
The Broken Point...11

Chapter Three
Delivering Me From Me...20

Chapter Four
When God Breaks You...27

Chapter Five
Why Does God Use The Broken?......................................33

Chapter Six
The Weakest Is The Strongest..43

Chapter Seven
The Potter Wants To Put You Back Together Again............52

Chapter Eight
There's Beauty In Brokenness...59

Chapter Nine
The Power Of Brokenness...67

Chapter Ten
Now I Surrender All...80

Conclusion..83

Chapter One

Face It Or Leave It

Life in Christ is not always what many people think it is.

It is not measured by how much of talent, strength and physical or mental endowment and capability one has, it is measured God's way and God's standard.

You don't come to Christ believing that your abilities can sustain you; no, you come relying in the strength of the Almighty.

And this is also true of your weaknesses.

So many people have put a blockage on their path to progress and strength with God because they price their strengths and abilities than the power of God.

So many other persons have stayed on a spot in the walk of faith because they groan and moan their weaknesses.

Unfortunately, either side of the coin is not good, and will not take you anywhere in the journey of faith.

Stop The Pretense

You have been running away from yourself, you have been putting the Spirit of God away from having the best of you because you have not come to face the real you - the main hindrance and enemy of your soul.

God cannot help you if you believe in yourself than you believe in Him. God cannot help you if you under value yourself too.

So, what are you to do?

Face the real problem, come to the end of self and God will help you.

How long are you going to pretend that you are right when you are wrong!

How long will you keep hiding your identity under the disguise of religion, it's time to come to terms with who you really are, to come to a broken point in life, where you take the Holy Spirit's reflection and assessment of self, so He can heal you.

When God Wants To Help You

The first step to deliverance is truth.

And when God wants to help you and change the course of your life, He gets you to see your true self and to accept the truth of who you are.

He causes you to stop hiding under the shadow by bringing you face to face with the enemy in you that needs to be dealt with.

The Bible is replete with men and women who were running away from who they really were, these people were a shadow of their true selves as far God was concerned.

But the way God went about healing and helping them was to first and foremost have them come to terms with who they really were.

In John Chapter 4, Jesus met a certain woman, a Samaritan woman, who was a shadow of herself.

Jesus knew that what she needed in life was true and enduring satisfaction that only God can give.

She was looking for all these things in men, but never got it.

When the Lord wanted to help and heal her, He had to first make her see who she really is, what her problem really was, what she has been hiding from.

"Jesus said to her, "Go, call your husband, and come here." The woman answered him, "I have no husband." Jesus said to her, "You are right in saying, „I have no husband"; for you have had five husbands, and the one you now have is not your husband. What you have said is true."
(John 4:16-18, ESV)

This dear woman was hungry for Life; though she didn't fully know what her real problem was at the time.

She was with the fifth man in her life, yet when Jesus said, "Go call your husband, and come here," she answered by saying; "I have no husband, even though she was living with a man at the moment."

Jesus didn't say to her, "you lied, you are with a man, that's your husband." Rather Jesus told her . she was correct.

It was at that point that she came to herself.

She left Jesus with Life and even had to go call others to drink of that Life.

Face it my dear; all these running around, inability to settle down is a result of an underlying problem.

You need true satisfaction that only Jesus gives.

But until you come to yourself, you may never be able to see your problem and then receive of the Lord, Water of Life, water that you drink once, and you'll never thirst again for the rest of life.

The Case Of Jacob

Now, a very basic and fundamental bible personality that we must refer to when dealing with the subject of brokenness is Jacob.

Jacob ran from His true self for years until one day.

How his name became Jacob in the first place, I don't know.

But that was who He is – a swindler, trickster, cheat, and deceiver.

He was this way for years and even had his father in-law – Laban, pay him back by deceiving him too into marrying Leah, the woman Jacob never planned he will marry.

Then came one day, when Jacob was at a crossroad, (the moment that will define his life), gripped with fear, and not knowing what exactly to do and what life holds afterwards, God showed up.

Thanks God that at his broken point, God showed up.

But God could not help Jacob until He first get Jacob to come to terms with his real self.

The way God did this was to ask him for his name: „And he said to him, "What is your name?" And he said, "Jacob." (Gen 32:27, ESV)

What is your name, the angel asked! Who are you; let's get down to examining your true self, nature, and identity?

And that was what got Jacob to face who He really was. So, what's your name?

Who are you?

What's that thing that you have been running away from, that thing that has been eating you up, that thing that has pushed into what you are doing you now?

Why do you have to make others pay for a sin that they never know anything about?

Why do you have to vent your anger on others just to repay an evil deed done to you by someone else?

Come to yourself, it's time to let God heal you.

But you must first accept that you are wrong, you are bad, you are no good, that you need help.

Why do you have to keep jumping from one man to another just because you want to torment your ex-husband?

Do you need to steal and make yourself a pseudo great life just to get at the lady who refused your advances?

Your motives are not right. You need a change.

So, what's your name, who are you! Now, God is reaching out to help you.

Healing is coming your way only that you must first accept that your style and motives are selfish, hurting and hating, then and only then can you get on your face and knee down before the Lord for purging, realigning and deliverance.

„Then he said, "Your name shall no longer be called Jacob, but Israel, for you have striven with God and with men, and have prevailed." " (Gen 32:28, ESV)

Oh, may the revelation of that Scripture hit you. It's deliverance for you today.

May the Spirit of the Lord convict you, bring you to see your true self, bring you to your knee where you'll ask the Lord to deliver and help you.

You cannot continue like this sir, you cannot continue to hide that hurt ma, staying under cover by getting yourself dirty some more.

It's time to come clean before the Lord and ask for a change.

It's the next phase of your life, and you cannot walk into it until you're changed by the Spirit. This is the only way to true and lasting impact.

It's time.

Realization By The Spirit

Nobody can get you to kneel; no one can help you come to this point of brokenness in life.

If for anything, pride will not allow you to even look at your true self and accept you for who you are.

But I have good news for you; the Spirit of the Lord can and will help you.

He's reaching out to you now; He's calling you to come kneel before Him where you can reason with Him.

Don't be too busy to ignore this call; don't put away this prompting by the Lord. Don't wait until you on the dying bed before you come to yourself.

You can still make the change now.

You know, humans are so strong and defensive that it takes only supernatural power to get them to break.

Man knows so much that he can hardly agree that he what he is except the power of the highest convicts him.

That's why our prayer today is that the Spirit of the Lord will be able to get through to you and get you down on you kneel where He needs you in the first place and thereon help you by changing you.

Don't resist the pull and the push of the Spirit; He loves you and wants to help you.

But in other to be able to do that, He must get you where you can surrender and ask His help. Listen to the voice of the Spirit now, let go and let God.

Please Face It; Don't Leave It

Our will are stubborn some many a times that it does stand in our way, hindering us from giving our all to God.

You know it, you and I have a weakness, that besetting nature, attitude that if not checked may destroy us.

Don't be shy about it; face it now and ask God to help you win over it.

It is not safe to put this over for another day; you may not know when your Master comes for your soul.

So now is the day, the real day to make the change.

What you don't destroy now, may end up destroying you tomorrow, therefore God is reaching out to you now to face it and deal with it.

Cast it before the Lord; that tobacco habits, that pornography thing, that lying habit, that money in your hand that you are using to oppress everyone who do not agree with you or say yes to your advances, cast it all before the Lord.

Let Him examine your motive, let God purify your heart and then fill you with heaven thereon.

You cannot continue to see another man's wife or husband; you cannot allow Satan to continue to use you to destroy and break homes.

Whatever the reason for it, (someone broke your own, so you must break other people's homes) is not good enough.

You must face it sir, face it ma, and deal with it.

You are just one step away from becoming all that heaven has created, planned, and redeemed you for, so why should you allow Satan and selfishness destroy God's purpose and grace in your life.

You are more than that, my friend.

God knows how to avenge your foes; He knows how to do it way much better than you do. You can't successfully do that job as much as God will do it.

He's master at it, you know!

So, it's time to face it, let go and then let God.

Why You Have Not Moved

See, the Spirit of God cannot move the uttermost and fill you with heaven if you keep the baggage of hate, pride, bitterness, revenge, envy, and un-forgiveness hanging in your life for that long.

Those are excess baggage that gets you stuck to a place so you cannot move with God.

The way to go is to put down the excess load at the feet of the Master and let Him give you, His burden.

And of course, Christ's yoke is easy, and His burden is light (Matthew 11:30)

Jacob blessed by His father Isaac and given the Blessing was still stuck until he came to himself and had the angel of the Lord blessed him again before even the prayer of his father Isaac will work for him.

It's that serious.

You are not experiencing the fullness of the Spirit in your life because you have not allowed the Spirit to breathe on you.

He's breathing on everything but it's not getting on you because you have literarily blocked the air with garbage.

Get these off your spirit so God can reach you with His breathe and blessing and turn the remaining days of your life around for good and greatness.

It's time to move.

Chapter Two

The Broken Point

Every one of us is strong one way or the other, strong will, strong body, fat bank account, great marriage and more.

But there's also something in us that is not strong, plus, even the strongest today can be become the weakest tomorrow when some things happen.

Unfortunately, most of us wait till the time we can't hold any more before we acknowledge that we need help.

But why wait till this critical moment before you sit with yourself and God, asking Him to check you, fix, heal and help you.

Well, the human nature, the stubbornness of man will not allow him to humble himself and ask for the help of God for the areas where he is supposedly strong and, in the areas, where he is the weakest.

No matter how strong you are, if God is not holding you, your strength might even destroy you. Ask Samson.

Strong as Samson was, he destroyed himself and his enemies with the same strength, but had he asked God for help even in his strongest moments, he would not have been in that mess.

Please watch your strength as much as you do your weaknesses.

You Need Help

The human nature and pride do not allow a lot of people to willingly surrender to the Lord, but somehow, a severe crisis in life makes us do so.

At that point, you know that if God does not come through for you, you are done for it.

You may even be experiencing one right now, you may be faced with the worst nightmare of your life.

It could be that your health is failing, and doctors have given up on you. Or that you have just been diagnosed of cancer or other incurable diseases.

And you know that if God does not help you, you are done for it.

Perhaps, your case may be a very serious marital crisis that is already threatening to end your marriage. Or any other family problem that can destroy your home, happiness, and joy.

What if your case is money problem, a desperate need for job that if you don't get one, you will lose your home, your comfort, and other things!

Yours may be a habitual and besetting sin. Have you ever come to a place in your life where you cry to God asking that if he does not deliver you from this sin or that sin, you cannot help it and are fixed for life?

We are talking about the broken point; where life situations and crisis force you to look up to God for help and deliverance.

I have been there!

This is the point where you know that you are drowning and desperately need rope or boards to cling to if you must survived.

I have been where it was all dark; life seems to be ebbing away, sins power seems to have the whole of me, yet I want to please God, I want to be the best I can be for God.

But I felt helpless, and I cried: „Lord, if you don't help me now, I can make it. Lord, if you don't save me, no one else can.

The Case OF The Apostle Paul

Apostle Paul was a great man of God in every respect and before he met the Lord on the way to Damascus, he was one of the best brains and strictest of Pharisee.

He loved God in his own way and was doing everything as a Pharisee to please God. Yet, Paul was in trouble; his flesh was having the best him, sin was eating him up.

He was literally taken captive by the desire of his body and could in way please God.

"For that which I do I allow not: for what I would, that do I not; but what I hate, that do I. If then I do that which I would not, I consent unto the law that *it is* good. Now then it is no more I that do it, but sin that dwelleth in me. For I know that in me (that is, in my flesh,) dwelleth no good thing: for to will is present with me; but *how* to perform that which is good I find not. For the good that I would I do not: but the evil which I would not, that I do. Now if I do that I would not, it is no more I that do it, but sin that dwelleth in me. I find then a law, that, when I would do good, evil is present with me. For I delight in the law of God after the inward man: But I see another law in my members, warring against the law of my mind, and bringing me into captivity to the law of sin which is in my members. O wretched man that I am! who shall deliver me from the body of this death?" (Romans 7:15-24, KJV)

Paul was in serious trouble, just like you and me.

He was not in control of his actions just like many of you are right now.

You found yourself stuck in that destructive pornographic habit and every now and then you pray, cry, and repent of it, but again and again, you found yourself back to it.

You have lost control even though you feel down and guilty every time you go that way, yet you are unable to completely break free however hard you try.

Brother, you need help.

And it is only God than can help you at this point.

Satan and sin have gotten the mastery of you, even though your spirit is crying to break free. You have become a prisoner to Satan, self and sin and are dying slowly, one punch after another. Sir, you are dying, you need help.

No Other Way To Go

You know it, there's no other way to go now but God.

So, it's time to cry out for His help and deliverance like a drowning man. But first you must come to the end of self.

Paul did and that was why he asked for help.

He was despicable; he knew it and acknowledged it.

He cried: "O wretched man that I am! Who shall deliver me from the body of this death?" Is that your cry right now?

If you are sincere and have finally come to the end of self, then there's help in God for you. You can breathe a sigh of relief, because there's help for you in Christ.

Sigh Of Relief

God has waited this long for you to come to this point, and now that you cry out for his help in desperation, He is ready to help.

Paul found help in Christ, you too will.

He shouted a response to the question he raised; „I thank God through Jesus Christ our Lord. " What a relief.

The grace of Jesus Christ is the answer and deliverance to your lifelong struggle. Grace and grace alone is the answer.

Now that you have quit trying to fight yourself, the grace of Christ is ready to take over. All you need do is to surrender.

Surrender all to grace, then healing and help will flow from the wounds of Christ right into your inner man bringing about deliverance.

How to Connect With This Grace

Thank God that you have come to the end of self.

Thank God that now you no longer believe in your strengths and will to help you.

Thank God even more that you have shouted your heart out to the Lord for help, so now is time to connect grace for help in this your desperate time of need.

Before I show how to connect grace, I like to show you what grace is.

Grace is God's ability prevailing over your inability. It is more than unmerited favor.

Grace is the power of God towering over your natural power. It is this power that breaks every yoke, delivers, and ends the fight in you once and for all.

When grace is flowing freely in your spirit, you do not have any struggle again, you do not have any fight to fight again. Rather, you just rest and glide with the Holy Spirit, the Spirit of liberty.

So now, let's get to it.

Here's how to connect grace for your deliverance.

1. By being alone with God.

The first thing that you must do when it comes to connecting grace to help in the time of your need is to get alone with God.

Go to a secluded place and seek God for help and release.

God likes it when you come looking and seeking Him for a definite need in your life.

The Bible says of Jacob when he came to the broken point in his life that „He was left alone." (Genesis 32:24)

He had to be left alone to face the ordeal of his life.

He had to be left alone to be able to think through on his problem.

He had to be left alone to come to a place of surrender where God can help him. He had to be left alone to see his true nature, trouble, and need.

He had to be left alone to come to the place in his life where he will acknowledge his weakness, and dependence on God.

He had to be left alone to come to the place where he will lay down his will and let God. He had to be left alone to face his shame and fear.

And when He was left alone, God met him, and blessed him. That is same and true for you, my friend.

2. To connect grace, you need to connect with the Spirit of Grace.

Grace is an ability, the ability of the Spirit of God.

And it is only the Holy Spirit that impacts and gives grace to the needy.

So, you have got to beckon on the Spirit of grace asking Him to come to your aid.

You have got to break your self-dependence and then acknowledge your total dependence on the Spirit of grace if you want to have and enjoy ceaseless and endless flow of grace in your life.

Grace is all you need; the Spirit of grace gives grace in abundance to as many that calls and asks for it.

So now is the time to reach out and call for the help of the Spirit and if you ask believing, you can be sure He will meet you right now and heal you completely.

"Ask, and it shall be given you; seek, and ye shall find; knock, and it shall be opened unto you: For everyone that asketh receiveth; and he that seeketh findeth; and to him that knocketh it shall be opened." (Matthew 7:7-8, KJV)

Do you believe the Scripture? Do you believe that?

Pray With Me Now:

Say; „Oh Lord my Father, I need your help. I have come to the end of myself. I need your grace. I found out Lord that I cannot help myself; and that no matter how hard I try, I keep failing. So, Lord, I ask that you help and deliver me now, in Jesus's name.

Holy Spirit of Grace, I ask for your grace right now. Please flow into my heart, spirit, soul, and body with the unceasing oil of grace. Make me strong within and without by your grace Lord and lift me to heights where I can no longer fall, in Jesus's name.

And thank you Father for answer to prayers, in Jesus' name. Amen!

Chapter Three
Delivering Me From Me

Your worst enemy is not the devil, it is not your boss, spouse, or your neighbor; the greatest enemy of your soul is the person you see in the mirror every time you look at the mirror.

You are your greatest enemy.

The Word of God is very clear on this; in short, Jesus made a very fundamental statement that borders on the evil that lives within man.

He said: "There is nothing from without a man, that entering into him can defile him: but the things which come out of him, those are they that defile the man." (Mark 7:15, KJV)

Simply stated, the worst evil that you must deal with is not those about people around you, but ones that are locked up within you.

Your carnal desires and passions, your un-renewed mind and untamed nature are the wickedest things about you.

He (Jesus) went further to explain it this way:

"Do ye not perceive, that whatsoever thing from without entereth into the man, *it* cannot defile him; Because it entereth not into his heart, but into the belly, and goeth out into the draught, purging all meats? And he said That which cometh out of the man, that defileth the man. For from within, out of the heart of men, proceed evil thoughts, adulteries, fornications, murders, Thefts, covetousness, wickedness, deceit, lasciviousness, an evil eye, blasphemy, pride, foolishness: All these evil things come from within, and defile the man." (Mar 7:18-23, KJV)

Don't tell me that you just beat up your wife suddenly out of the provocation. No! You must have been thinking about what you are going to do to her all this while she has been provoking you.

And today, you finally executed your thought, you beat her up.

People who commit crime with capital offense like rape, murder, suicide, and robbery do not just do it suddenly; these acts are calculated, planned, and executed.

It comes to you as a suggestion from hell; you bought into it, gave yourself to it and then through careful and proper planning executed it.

„Out of the heart comes out every evil thought, " Jesus said.

Now the heart is the real you, your spirit that which makes you who you are.

What Paul Said About Evil Passion

Now, you would think some things that we do are caused by Satan, or that we are under the direct influence of Satan when doing them, but the Bible said something different.

Now the works of the flesh are manifest, which are *these;* Adultery, fornication, uncleanness, lasciviousness, Idolatry, witchcraft, hatred, variance, emulations, wrath, strife, seditions, heresies, Envying, murders, drunkenness, reveling, and such like: of the which I tell you before, as I have also told *you* in time past, that they which do such things shall not inherit the kingdom of God.
(Galatians 5:19-21, KJV)

You would have thought that envy, strife, and drunkenness are the works of Satan. You would even think that fornication, adultery, hatred, and witchcraft are works of the devil. But the Bible calls them the works of the flesh, the manifestation of your own body.

These things are things that the carnal mind and body takes pleasure in doing. It is you that are doing them and not the devil.

So, who is to blame for your lust and love for married women even though you yourself are married!

It is you and not the devil.

Acknowledging the Cause

If there's anything God loves, it is honesty and sincerity.

God will always show His mercy to those who admit that they have problem and cannot help themselves.

So, the part to deliverance will be first and foremost to acknowledge that the greatest problem you must deal with is you, yourself, appetites, and passions.

Now, God already knows that you have these problems but until He can get you to the place where you will admit that you have them, He cannot help you.

So, it is enlightened self-interest to admit your weakness before the Lord asking Him to help you. That's the point where His grace will be released for your deliverance.

Until you look yourself in the mirror and point to you and say, „hey dude, you are the enemy of my soul and I want to get rid of you now," you may not make it through the problem of self.

Deliverance From Self

Hallelujah, God has made provision for your deliverance in Christ.

The basis for your deliverance is the finished work of Christ on the cross; where you died to self and then self-died to you.

On the cross, you died to the world and the world died to you.

And then when Jesus rose again from the dead, you rose with Him - a new man, one that has triumphed over the flesh, sin, Satan, and the world.

You already have the victory; you have the dominion in Christ.

Now, all you need to do is to appropriate your victory in Christ over the flesh and to accept by faith what Jesus has done for you and then wait in place of prayer to activate God's grace over that self.

Grace is God's mightiest delivering power, whenever you have a thorn in your flesh; grace will take care of it if you acknowledge the problem and asked God for deliverance.

And here's something you should know about God's grace: Grace, God's redeeming grace is always enough.

At one point in the Apostle Paul's life, he needed help to overcome satanic persecution and troubles that trailed him from the time he got saved even to the end of his ministry.

After so much praying and waiting, Jesus told him that He has given him grace - that His grace is more than enough – sufficient and that his strength is made perfect in weakness.

That's the same thing God is giving you now.

His grace is always more than enough for you, and His power works best and finds its full expression in your weaknesses.

Ask and receive God's grace now.

And here's what to expect when grace is released, and you have received it.

1. You will be surprised that the desire and reckless drive for that evil has just vanished.

2. You will find out that the guilt that those evils have heaped on your heart has just lifted. You just don't feel the guilt and the condemnation anymore.

3. You will suddenly find that songs of praise and thanksgiving for God's forgiveness, love and mercy have filled your heart.

4. You heart will be filled with fresh love for people and your eyes will be filled with holy looks and passion.

5. You will see that you are now ready to help people instead of hurting them.

6. You will be shocked at the change and power you will begin to see in your prayer life.

7. You will begin to experience a level of endurance and tolerance you have never had before. You will choose to suffer, if need be, rather than to hurt people.

These and more are some of the characteristics of a grace filled soul.

I needed to highlight some of them here for you so that you will be able to measure your life, the deliverance and the change that has come to you.

When Jesus visits you with grace, you will and should know of course.

Keeping The Devil Out

Now, I want to quickly remind you of something: because you have received grace and freedom does not mean that you will not be tempted again.

In short, Satan will come all out against you to make you destroy your deliverance by yourself. Now, what you need do is to learn how to resist him.

But first, you must learn how to not give him place in your life again. Do not yield again to his lures and lies again.

You must again receive grace to resist him when he comes with his lures again and you must receive grace to not give him any place in your life again.

You see; your fight with self and Satan, your victory over them is all by grace. And your continued victory is also by the same grace.

Therefore grace, grace and grace is all you need to win and keep winning.

Receive grace, in Jesus's name. Amen!

Chapter Four

When God Breaks You

At a point in our lives, we all experience brokenness though each case may be different.

For some people, they come to their broken point after a long wooing by the Holy Spirit. But for some others, it comes sudden, God breaking into your realm, getting you down of your knee.

Either way, the results that come from this encounter with God is always dramatic and long lasting.

But I want us to particularly look at cases when God breaks you. What will happen and what will become of you.

The Case Of The Apostle Paul

Stubborn, strong willed, defiant but in ignorance, the young Paul went about doing all that he could do against the Christian faith and their Jesus in the early Church.

In short, he said in an account that he was ready to do anything contrary and against the name of Jesus. (Acts 26:9)

But good for old Paul, God broke him.

"And Saul, yet breathing out threatening and slaughter against the disciples of the Lord, went unto the high priest, And desired of him letters to Damascus to the synagogues, that if he found any of this way, whether they were men or women, he might bring them bound unto

Jerusalem. And as he journeyed, he came near Damascus: and suddenly there shined round about him a light from heaven: And he fell to the earth, and heard a voice saying unto him, Saul, Saul, why persecutest thou me? And he said, Who art thou, Lord? And the Lord said, I am Jesus whom thou persecutest: *it is* hard for thee to kick against the pricks. And he trembling and astonished said, Lord, what wilt thou have me to do? And the Lord *said* unto him, Arise, and go into the city, and it shall be told thee what thou must do." (Acts 9:1-6, KJV)

I will that God will do what He did to the apostle Paul to as many of His choice children who are still going their way, heading their direction, and doing everything for their own selfish gain.

How long will you keep on having your plans and living for yourself?

God wants you to not just serve Him but to He wants you to live your all for Him. Maybe I should ask you a question: "what and who are you living for; self or God?"

Are you living for the praise of man or of God? What drives

you every day? Is it money, fame, power or what?

Like little old Paul before He met the Lord, he lived for self or rather for what he believed was just and right.

But what about when God broke him, he found out that all that he was living for was completely opposite to what he was created for and should be living for.

Are you that way?

Realization

Paul went about wreaking havoc in the body of Christ, one day on his way to Damascus for the same cause, the Lord Jesus met him and broke him.

„Saul, Saul" (as he was called then), a voice from the midst of light shouted out his name. That got him.

His identity was challenged by the voice, and he was shocked to have someone call his name in the middle of the day from within a light brighter than the sun

„Why are you persecuting me," the voice said.

Startled and bewildered by the question; Paul said, „who are you Lord that I persecute?"

„I am Jesus who you are persecuting," the Lord replied. „You cannot be playing with a scorpion's tail and don't get bitten," the Lord added.

Now the next verse is something I really wanted you to see.

It says, „And he trembling and astonished said, Lord, what wilt thou have me to do?" The Lord broke Paul.

He was dazed, shocked, frightened, and humbled.

Do you need the Lord to deal with you that way before you respond to Him?

Do you need to have the Lord throw you to the ground and take your sight off for 3 days before you come humbling yourself in repentance?

Well, if He must, He will do it. (All for your good, you know).

But you better be prepared for the blindness and the throwing to the ground.

Better still, you better be prepared to ask Him the right question when this happens.

The Change

Dazed and startled beyond measure, Paul asked the Lord for what He was to do. And that was the right thing to do, you know.

What would you expect of a man whose sight was perfect a few minutes ago and just in another minute got blinded?

He would certainly want the way out.

This is the call, this is where God wants to get you, the place where you will humble yourself, put your plans and pursuits aside and then ask Him for his plan for your life.

God wants you in the place where you will ask Him what you should do with your wealth, time, body, strength, education, and all now.

When God breaks you, that's the time to give up your drive, ask for His plan and go for it.

When God breaks you

You do not have to really wait for the hammer of God to come on you before you humble yourself and ask for God's grace.

But if God must do it to get you, so be it.

But when God breaks you, here are some things that you get.

1. When God breaks you, He takes you from a sinner to a saint
2. When God breaks you, He changes your vision and your direction
3. When God breaks you, He takes the pride and self away.
4. When God breaks you, He humbles you with a temporarily pain
5. When God breaks, He gets you up and fortified you for a brand-new future
6. When God breaks you, He fires you up and makes you strong for the troubles ahead

7. When God breaks you, He turns you into His priced servant and messenger of His grace.

A lot comes with the breaking of the Lord, so much that you may want to ask for a breaking right now at will.

But you know, God's anvil and hammer do not come when you need it, God comes when He has given you time enough to change and repent at will.

He knows your heart; He knows that even if you are asking for Him to break you now because you are reading this book, your motives are not pure and right yet.

So, He keeps wooing you by the Spirit to willingly surrender to His love and mercy, but when you bluntly refuse and refute the Spirit, He will get at you still in love but with a cane to beat and leave an indelible mark on you that you will never forget for the rest of life.

God's love is kind, it is patient, yet it is severe.

In all, when God breaks you, He makes you again into His best, the very image of Christ. Do you want some breaking!

Say; „Yes Lord! I need you to break me and make me for your glory. "

„Break me Lord, " in Jesus' name. Amen!

Chapter Five

Why Does God Use The Broken?

God is amazing and incomprehensible.

I bet you, you cannot fully explain God, yes, you can explain some things about Him, but there are yet many more things that cannot be explained about God.

Now, can you explain why God loves you, can anybody successfully explain the love and the grace of God?

Not you and not me.

We may know a glimpse here and there of God, but we truly are not able to understand His motives, the real reason why He does the things He does.

And not only you, but even Satan too does also not know and cannot comprehend God.

The Scriptures said that Had Satan knew (God's motive and end point) as far redemption of humanity is concerned, he would not have crucified the Lord of glory – talking about the crucifixion of Christ. (1 Corinthians 2:8)

Satan was mad about Christ and His acts and thought that the way to stop Him was to get rid of Him by killing him.

At the end he didn't know that he was doing God's cause – he was helping to bring about your redemption, which of course was his doom.

So, Satan used his hand to destroy himself- to cause his own eternal doom when he had Jesus killed.

You see, if he had some inkling as to what was going to be the end of the game; he would not have toll that path.

Unfortunately, the deed has been done. Your redemption and my deliverance have been accomplished; you are free, and I am free. And the devil has lost it.

What would you say?

This is called the wisdom of God

The Wisdom of God

The reason why God uses the broken has everything to do and to say about His wisdom. God alone can fully explain that?

In the broken body of Christ on the cross, God's wisdom secures your healing – by the wounds of Christ, you are cured.

In the shed blood of Christ, His body ripped, and blood ceaselessly flowed out, His heart ruptured with blood and water gushed out from the piercing of the sword on His side by that soldier, your sins are forgiven and remitted legally and eternally.

God used the broken body and heart of Christ to deliver and secure our redemption.

That's God for you, He specializes in using broken vessels for His utmost so that no man will glory in his strength. (2 Corinthians 12:5-10)

God is so amazing and beautiful that He delights in things that the natural human wisdom does not pride and take delight in.

Have you ever asked yourself; how tall and body built was Samson? What about David and his mighty men, did you think they were giants, very tall, well-built, and muscular?

Not so.

These people were ordinary people, with average height and strength. They were not people you would consider the mighty. No, they were just like you and me.

But the wisdom of God was to take this simple ordinarily people and then filled them with divine supernatural strength to do feats for Him.

These men under the influence of the Spirit were unpredictable and unconquerable.

But when the Spirit of the Lord is not on them, you could easily tie them up (like Samson), slap their faces and have them killed.

These men were not physically strong; they were only strong in God. And in the strength of God, they did wonders that baffled the ancient world and are still the talk of our word today.

Such is the wisdom of God.

So Why Does God Use The Broken Really

In the wisdom of God, though we cannot explain why he does some things, yet we have some inkling here and there that we can allude to as to some of the reasons why He uses the broken.

1. The Broken Have Lost Confidence in their Ability Completely

One of the reasons why God uses broken people is because they have completely lost ability in themselves.

That language of the broken is „Lord, without you I can do nothing. " They don't believe they can, they only believe God can through them. The broken does not have, God has.

The broken is not self-made, but God made.

Therefore, the idea of self-made millionaires does not fly with me as a Christian.

The Christian who is broken is not self-made, but God made. He knows it and talks that way.

God use the broken like Paul because they always acknowledge their weaknesses, submitting it to God. That way they allow God to put His strength in them and do His thing the way He wants.

Have you come to the end of self?

Do you still have confidence in what you can do because of your high-level proficiency, skills, and education?

It's okay to have all that.

But if you want God to use you, you must first come to the end of all that. Then acknowledge God above them and He will move you on from there.

2. The Broken Are Dependent On God Fully

Oh, if there's anything that the broken does is that they fully depend on God.

They allude everything to God – in God they move, live, and have their being. (Acts 17:28) When they sleep and wake up, it is God. When they go out and come back, it is God.

When they fly or stumble, it is all God.

These people have learned the secret of utter dependence on God; everything they do and have been all Gods".

They can never claim anything but God. (1 Corinthians 15:10, Colossians 1:29) God loves these kinds of people.

3. Nobody Takes The Glory

Another reason why God uses the broken is because God wants to take and have the glory in all things.

"For ye see your calling, brethren, how that not many wise men after the flesh, not many mighty, not many noble, *are called*: But God hath chosen the foolish things of the world to confound the wise; and God hath chosen the weak things of the world to confound the things which are mighty; And base things of the world, and things which are despised, hath God chosen, *yea*, and things which are not, to bring to naught things that are: That no flesh should glory in his presence." (1 Corinthians 1:26-29, KJV)

God's glory, honor and praise is something He will never share with anybody.

So, when you have the tendencies to claim that you are the one doing the things, making things happen, God will never use you.

But when you have come to the end in yourself and believe God is all there is, you don't take glory for gains, victories, and feats; you give all the glory to the Lord.

And seeing that the broken are this way; that is why God always uses them.

You will never hear the apostle Paul takes glory for all that he accomplished for God. Rather, he would say it is the grace of God that did it through him.

Crushed, broken, and then remade and raised by the Lord, he knew that he can never say that he did, but that God did.

4. Because They Have Surrendered

The number one characteristic of the broken is „surrender."

A broken person is one who had fought and argued and try all and then after a while came to a point of surrender – the point where he says, „Lord, all of you and none of me."

The person who has surrendered to the Lord, who has given up all his glorified strengths and abilities and who also has given up all his shameful weaknesses is the very friend of God.

This person will be used of God.

In short, the Bible says that God dwells in eternity and that He also dwells with the lowly in heart and those of a contrite spirit.

God's manifest presence is not revealed in every heart as it were, but God manifests and finds His permanent dwelling with the broken.

What about that?

"For thus says the One who is high and lifted up, who inhabits eternity, whose name is Holy: "I dwell in the high and holy place, and with him who is of a contrite and lowly spirit, to revive the spirit of the lowly, and to revive the heart of the contrite." (Isa 57:15, ESV)

The great God who lives in eternity also finds the heart of the lowly and contrite a pleasant place to dwell. And He does this for one main purpose; to revive their spirits and hearts.

It is amazing the places where God chooses to be found.

And it is much more amazing what He chooses to do in and with such places.

The Humble and Contrite

The humble and the contrite are broken-hearted for their sins.

They are the ones humble enough to be penitent for the evil they have done, asking God to forgive and to have mercy upon them.

These are deeply affected with grief and godly sorrow for having offended God. They are the ones who are ready to do restitution even to people they have cheated and stolen from before they came to know the Lord.

The contrite knows how to repent.

King David of Israel was a very good example of a person who knows how to repent and repent quickly by taking responsibility for his own wrongdoing.

King David will never blame a third party for his sin (King Saul was that way), but rather when confronted with his failures, admitted quickly, repented, and asked God for help.

Are you quick to repent of your sins?

Or do you play the blame game anytime the Lord is convicting you of your failures.

You had better learn to be a person who is quick to repent, one who truly feels sorry for sins every time and any time.

If you are this way, then God is at home in you. You're the type of person He wants to permanently reside in his heart and body.

You are the type of person that God can trust and use.

You are the type of person that the Lord will not be hesitant to trust with power and authority.

When God knows that you will return all the glory to Him, you will never claim you did anything but Him and that you will continue to depend on Him for everything and anything, then God is set to come down on you with His Spirit of grace and power, fill you with all of Himself and then use you for His glory.

Above all, when God sees you fit to bear His name, He will then use your hurt and the things you have learnt from them to heal others.

You become the best qualified to represent the Lord in your place of calling.

Did you see what you stand to gain when you let the Lord break you or when you voluntarily yield to the wooing of the Spirit to come to repentance?

So, what are you going to do now?

Surrender or hold on still in your strong will, pride, and arrogance? That decision is up to you.

But the gains are too much to overlook or look away. Choose wisely my friend.

Chapter Six
The Weakest Is The Strongest

The hardest thing for humans to do is to live the surrendered life. It is so hard because of the power of the flesh.

The flesh does not want you to forgive, it does not want you to let go.

In short, the flesh tells you that letting go and forgiving the person who hurts you makes you a weakling.

It tells you that you are a coward, that's why you are chickening out of the situation.

It gives you reasons to not let go, to defend yourself and to be man and pay back to prove that you're courageous, bold, and strong.

This is the way of the flesh.

But if you must win the battle over the flesh and have yourself approved for God's work and use, then you must overcome the flesh.

What's the Flesh?

Now, understand that your body is not the same as the flesh as it were in scriptures.

In short, your body, the Bible says, is the temple of the Holy Spirit and it is therefore holy. (1 Corinthians 3:16-17, 6:15-20)

But that is different from your flesh.

Your flesh stands for the members of the body.

That is your tongue, eyes, nose, hands, mind, eyes, emotions etc.

These are regarded as the members of the body.

Did you ever realize that when the Holy indwells a person, He goes for the person's tongue first? This is because the tongue is the most critical part of your members.

A lot depends on it; it can kill, and it can make alive.

It is the control room for the whole of your body and the members, and it is the control room for your success as a Christian and for your failure too (it all depends on how you use it).

These members of the body are the things you are to deal with to have the mastery over the flesh and then to be able to bring yourself to the place where God can break, make, and use you.

The five senses of the body feed the mind information; the mind then processes it and gives its back for use.

If the mind is not renewed by the word of God, it processes the perceived information and comes with final analytical data that are devilish and satanic.

When the mind is not renewed, revenge is the king of the rules. When the mind is not renewed, pride is the other of the day.

When the mind is not renewed, gain, self-satisfaction, power, and wealth are the main thing.

And you can do anything to achieve your dream when the mind is dirty, set and hardened by the devil for evil.

Therefore, one of the greatest needs of the Church today is the renewal of the mind. Next to the power of the un-renewed mind is the passion of the sense of touch.

Therefore, many people are slaves to the devil today.

They are people who want to gratify the flesh, love to touch and feel.

These senses must be really dealt with if you want to get to the broken point in life and sustain it afterwards.

What about the eyes?

This one is as deadly as the others if not harnessed. It even helps to inflame the sense of touch.

You see before you touch.

You see, the mind takes the information, process it, and gives it back to you with a response which is touch.

These senses are really the true enemy of man and not Satan as it. So, what do you do to the flesh or the members of your body now? Crucify it.

How to Crucify The Flesh

This is a hard thing really for many people to do because of the power and stronghold that the flesh has built in them overtime.

But it is easy by the Spirit.

So, but what does it mean to crucify the flesh. It simply means to „deny it of pleasure. "

It is the disciplining of the members of the body to conform to the word of God. Anything can be disciplined you know.

You can train your flesh to obey God "sword, to respond to only righteousness and holiness.

"And they that are Christ's have crucified the flesh with the affections and lusts." (Galatians 5:24)

The beautiful thing about the Christian faith is that all things that you will ever need to overcome in life have been provided for by the blood of Christ.

In Christ, you have already died to the flesh; you just only need to put into practice what you have already gotten.

Just go ahead and tame the members of your body, they don't have power enough to resist the taming.

God has empowered you to tame the flesh in that in Christ He has already stripped all the members the dominating, demanding and inflaming power and passion.

The flesh has no absolute unbreakable power over you, you have all the power over it. Take responsibility and do something g about it.

"But I discipline my body and keep it under control, lest after preaching to others I myself should be disqualified." (1Corinthians 9:27, ESV)

Yes, you can keep your body under control; you can discipline it and make it do what you want. Now, here are few ways to discipline your flesh.

1. Deny it

A lot of people live for today and the gratification of the now, no delay at all.

No, if you want to learn to start to discipline your body, you must learn to consciously deny it of its immediate desires and passions.

In short, maturity, they say, is the ability to delay gratification.

Take for instance you are supposed to eat heavily by 8pm before you go to bed. In short, this has been your routine.

Now, you want to train your body to a different routine.

What do you do; instead of eating heavy by 8pm, eat something light.

You can be sure that you may not be able to sleep and sleep very well the first few nights you start to do this.

But because you have a purpose for what you are doing it and because your will is empowered by the Spirit, you tell yourself you will eat otherwise.

And that you will not die before the morning comes, so with resolve you go through it.

If you do that for one week, you will discover that your body will begin to reset and adjust to the new routine.

And for 21 days is what it normally takes to break and to make old and new habit, (because

that's how much it will take for your body to adjust well to the change), soon you will look back and will be shocked at the change.

Fasting is a way to discipline the flesh, you know.

Fast not only your dinner or breakfast, fast your TV also.

Tell yourself that you will not stay watching TV for 8 hours a day; that from now, you will reduce watch time to 5 hours, while the other 3 hours will now go for prayer and study of the word.

It may not be easy the first few days, but with your will set and empowered by the Spirit, you can.

Get to discipline the members of your body consciously. Train them in the way of Christ, the way of the new creation and in no time, they will start to do what you want exactly.

After all, the body is to serve the spirit and not the spirit being a slave to the body.

In Christ, your spirit now born again has been empowered by the Holy Spirit to have the control and dominion over the body, its members and even the soul.

2. Talk to it

Another way to tame the members of the flesh is to continually talk to the body.

If you are born again and filled with the Holy Spirit and speaking in tongues, your tongue is anointed.

The power of the Holy Spirit is released from within you through the tongue into any area of the body, into any situations and circumstances you want to effect a change.

Talk to your body; tell it what you want and how you want it.

Demand obedience from that member of the body and it will obey you.

I tell you the truth, your human spirit indwelled and anointed by the Holy Spirit can control, tame and trained the members of the body by talking to it.

Remember it is not just you are talking, and you are not also talking your own words, it the Spirit of God in union with your recreated human spirit that is talking, and it is the word of God that you are declaring.

And where the word of a king is, there's power. (Ecclesiastes 8:4) God's word is God's power. (Romans 1:16)

The Place of the Spirit

Now, to end this chapter, let me quickly add that your victory over the flesh will come by the Spirit of Grace.

So, you have got to befriend the Spirit.

Sincerely tell the Holy Spirit what the challenges are and always ask Him to help you.

The Holy Spirit is the one that works out the victory of the cross of Christ in the individual believer.

So, without Him, there's no victory, and there's no winning.

But to have Him go to work in you and for you, you must learn to always acknowledge Him and depend on Him completely.

So do not ignore the Holy Spirit if you want to win.

You cannot ignore your wife or husband for a day and stay in happy fellowship with him or her. The Holy Spirit is no different.

You need not ignore Him for one day. You must fellowship Him every day.

The Christian life without the fellowship of the Spirit is dried, boring, a struggle, weak and a total failure.

I just saved you now.

So, go start to learn to treat the Holy Spirit well and daily as you would you spouse every day if you don't want to risk quarrel, rift and contention with her or him?

All the best!

Chapter Seven
The Potter Wants To Put You Back Together Again

I love how the Lord walks with us; the way He gets His purpose accomplished in your life is not something you can fathom.

If God asks you to sit down and plan out the way your very life will go and turn out in Christ in the next 10 years, you will be shocked that what you'll have will be completely different from His!

This is because God's way and plans are higher than your ways and His thoughts than your thought. (See Isaiah 55:8-9)

In your little mind, you may be able to figure out, plan and project that your life will go a certain direction based on some facts that are available to you now.

Now, no matter how accurate and factual those factors are, they are way too low than the ways of God. And they are subject to change.

Therefore, the Scripture says: *"But as it is written, Eye hath not seen, nor ear heard, neither have entered into the heart of*

man, the things which God hath prepared for them that love him. But God hath revealed them unto us by his Spirit: for the Spirit searcheth all things, yea, the deep things of God."
(1 Corinthians 2:9-10, KJV)

You see, God's plan for you, the way He wants you go and turn out in life is something you cannot figure out yourself right now. But they come by progressive revelation through the Spirit.

Your life is unveiled one step at a time as you begin to walk in obedience to the Spirit of God.

Now here's what I want you to see - how God works this purpose out in your life – the making process.

The Rebrand

Now, when God had you in the place where you have completely surrendered, your broken point, then He takes on from there and brands you into a new product that's completely fitted for His service and glory.

God takes you through His manufacturing factory, where He breaks you, makes and redesigns you into a finished product, a vessel unto honor.

This remaking is the turning point for every broken person.

Therefore, broken people always turn out to become fire for God, ministers of hope, love, and life for God.

Out of their brokenness, God makes them into new vessels

that carry His glory. That accounts for the reason why God uses the broken.

They have completely surrendered to the Lord, throw themselves at the mercy of the Lord, stopped to struggle with the Lord, then the Lord will see fit to remake them and use them for His praise.

This is what God wants to do with your life. He wants to remake you, having broken you.

"The word that came to Jeremiah from the LORD: "Arise, and go down to the potter's house, and there I will let you hear my words." So, I went down to the potter's house, and there he was working at his wheel. And the vessel he was making of clay was spoiled in the potter's hand, and he reworked it into another vessel, as it seemed good to the potter to do." (Jeremiah 18:1-4, ESV)

At the point where you are broken, you become like the clay that was marred in the hand of the potter.

And then the potter (God) at that instance reworked you into another vessel, one that is pleasing to Him, one that seems fit for Him to do.

Now, here are some things you should know about this creation process:

1. The Potter (Maker) is God

2. The clay is you

3. The clay does not decide for the potter what it is to be made into.

4. The clay does not argue with the potter as to what it wants to be made into during the making process.

5. The potter makes the clay into what seems good to him.

6. The potter reworks the clay into a different vessel that He started out with in the first place.

7. The potter takes full responsibility for what He creates/recreates.

You see, that's the process that makes the broken into what they eventually become.

And because you are not the potter, you can hardly figure out what He will make you into.

But because God is good, His workmanship created in Christ Jesus (you) will no doubt be the best.

...And because God creates for a purpose and ultimately for His glory, your life will turn out to be for the praise and the glory of His name in the long run.

So let that sink and settle in your heart; God is reworking you for His ultimate; the praise and glory of His name.

Make sure you don't struggle, argue, or dictate with the potter in the making process. He knows what is good and best and that's what he will make you into.

You can trust the Lord!

A New Creation

Did you ever notice that at salvation, God makes something entirely new out of you; He makes you a new creation.

God can never use you until He has reworked you.

He changed your nature at salvation into the nature of Christ, imparted His life and righteousness into you and then recreates your spirit man to be a new one, one that has never existed before.

That's always the process.

Then as you begin to grow and to walk with the Lord, He begins to make you and fit you into the very image of Christ.

That's the way the Lord deals with all His loved ones.

This is the way He deals with you until you stand perfect and complete in all His will.

He does this at every junction and major turn of your life, so be ready to be broken every time God is ready to take you on to a new level.

This is the way of the Lord.

Your Perfection and Completeness

Don't you ever make the mistake of thinking that the breaking process of God is just once, no God breaks you every time He needs to make something amazing out of you again.

Yes, the major turning point may be the very first brokenness (like the one of Paul on his way to Damascus), but afterwards Paul had to be broken again and again by the Lord until he completely fit into God's purpose and agenda.

God will not stop to break you until you become complete and perfect in Him.

Yes though, the breakings or subsequent breaking may not be as tough as the first and major one but all the way, God will be working and reworking you until you become complete in Christ.

Sorry, this may take a lifetime, but it is all for your good.

So, brothers and sisters, submit yourself, will and all to the Lord, let Him pound and break you a hundred times if He must, let Him rework you into vessels of whatever form and shape per time, but be sure that the end of the journey will be one of praise, glory, and grace.

Allow Him

The Potter may have put you back into some form yesterday or some months ago, but if you are not fully fitted, He will have to do it again.

And again, He will do it until you become.

So, make up your mind to allow God's making process to continue in you.

Allow the Lord to prune, re-prune and cut to size your very

self until you come out a most desirable and adorable vessel that the whole world will be all out for.

This is the will of God; this is the purpose of God.

So do not resist God's purpose until He has completely made you. The Potter wants to put you back together again.

Pray With Me:

Oh Lord my Father, I yield my all to you, I submit my all to you, I throw myself with utter abandonment at your mercy and love. Make me Lord into your best, fill me completely into your image and take all the glory.

In Jesus name! Amen!

Chapter Eight
There's Beauty In Brokenness

The most beautiful thing that may happen to a Christian is to be broken.

This is something that we may as well learn from the life of the Lord Jesus Himself. What was it that makes the life of the Son of God so amazing and beautiful?

It was the fact that Jesus understood what brokenness is and lived the broken life and practiced its lifestyle all through His walk and ministry on earth.

Was Jesus dependent on the Father completely?

Yes! You will hear Him say every now and then; „I can of my own self do nothing, as I hear so I judge. " (John 5:30)

Did Jesus surrender His all to the Father? Yes, He did.

You hear Him say; "Father, not my will but your will be done." (Matthew 26:39)

He never came to do His own thing, but the things of the Father, the things that the Father commanded Him.

Jesus is the true picture of brokenness.

Of course, He is God's perfect example and model for your life and my life. It is in Christ that we truly see the beauty of brokenness.

Now, let us see some things that makes brokenness most beautiful

1. Assumption

Now, the term assumption means several things, but in our context, assumption means to take full responsibility for another.

In the life of Christ, we see that Father God took complete responsibility for everything Jesus did and spoke.

Not only that, but the Father also took responsibility for His resurrection too. That is serious.

Did you realize that Jesus would not have been able to raise Himself from the dead?

God had to undertake to do that, to raise Him from the dead through the power of the Holy Spirit.

Why will God not suffer His holy one to see corruption?

One of the reasons was because His Holy One was completely obedient and dependent on Him.

When you have come to surrender your all to the Lord, He assumes responsibility for your life and for your death.

Nothing that happens to you will be a product of chance or happenstance, no. Your life and living becomes the responsibility of God and you and I know that when God takes responsibility for a thing, there will never be any dereliction of duty.

God never fails in His duty and when He takes responsibility for you, then you can rest assure that you are made for life.

Now, the one thing that brings you to this point is brokenness and complete dependence upon the Lord.

You can never pay your bills when God takes responsibility for your life. You don't fear death when God assumes responsibility for your life.

You are not afraid of tomorrow when God undertake to fully assume responsibility for you. This is what brokenness does to you, my brother.

You have abandoned yourself to the Lord completely; and He has assumed your all completely.

You never carry any load again for time again, you never worry, fret or care because you know the Lord cares for you, has taken responsibility for your welfare and warfare.

Praise the Lord, brokenness is beautiful.

2. Defense

Another beautiful thing that makes the broken life amazing is that God takes over the protection of your life, soul, ministry, and family.

This is important, so I must mention it separately from assumption.

Now, did you ever read in the scripture how that God the trinity jealously defend and protect the Holy Spirit? (See Matthew 12:31-32)

Because of the nature of the Holy Spirit (tender, harmless and loving, easily retrieves in sadness when wounded), the Father and the Son takes it upon themselves to protect and defend Him. (See Isaiah 63:10)

That's serious.

God does not like it when the Spirit is wounded or injured and saddened. So, He protects Him with utmost care.

That's the same way; the Lord protects the broken in Him.

He knows they are incapable of protecting themselves, so He takes on their defense for life. That's another beautiful grace that the broken enjoys from the Lord.

Don't you like it!

3. Transformation

There's a working of the Spirit of God in the life of the broken that results in complete transformation.

When a person is penitent, repents and allows God to have His way completely in his life, there's a complete change in that person.

By repentance the Spirit of God can work freely in that person's heart and body impacting the very life of the Son of God in its fullness.

God so want to work in us and through us, His Spirit who is the agent and communicator of the divine life wants to walk and work in you infiltrating your entire being with His life.

Yet a lot of us are not able to experience this moving and working of the Spirit. This is because we are not broken.

For when you are broken, your inner recesses become free and open for the free flow of the glory of God bringing transformation in your life from one level of glory to another by the Spirit of God. (See 2 Corinthians 3:18)

The rivers of God's Spirit can flow through every part of your being unhindered. The result is complete transformation – spirit, soul, and body.

This was the way the Life of Lord was.

4. Exaltation

Jesus again is the perfect example of the beauty of brokenness as far being exalted is concerned.

In Philippians 2:5-11, the Scripture charges bus to have the mindset of Christ and then showed us what this mindset was all about and what He got for this type of mindset in the long run.

"Let the same disposition be in you which was in Christ Jesus. Although from the beginning He had the nature of God He did not reckon His equality with God a treasure to be tightly

grasped. Nay, He stripped Himself of His glory, and took on Him the nature of a bondservant by becoming a man like other men. And being recognized as truly human, He humbled Himself and even stooped to die; yes, to die on a cross. It is in consequence of this that God has also so highly exalted Him, and has conferred on Him the Name, which is supreme above every other, in order that in the Name of JESUS every knee should bow, of beings in Heaven, of those on the earth, and of those in the underworld, and that every tongue should confess that JESUS CHRIST is LORD, to the glory of God the Father." (Weymouth)

The broken are lifted and exalted by God.

You can never find them where they were before they got broken.

No, the Lord cleanses them, remakes them and then lifts them to places of honor and glory.

Have you never read that God raises the poor from the dust and the beggar from the dunghill and then set them among princesses, the princesses of His people? And that He also cause them to inherit thrones of glory (See 1 Samuel 2:8)

The broken is the poor in spirit, the contrite in heart; God always exalts such. (Matthew 5:3)

Jesus' today is exalted to the right hand of the Father where He sits to govern the universe with the word of His power.

All this because He humbled Himself, depended on God for everything.

God always rewards the lowly and crushed in spirit with exaltation when they turn to Him.

5. Authority

Did you ever wonder why Jesus has so much authority today in heaven, earth, and hell?

It was because He went down, got broken before the Lord, then God exalted Him and gave Him authority far above any other authority in the 3 worlds of heaven, earth, and hell.

God has not changed; He gives and permits the exercise of authority to as many as are broken. Now, brokenness makes God to trust you.

He knows you have come to the end of self; So, He begins to allow you to touch and exercise power beyond the ordinary so much so that the world around you will wonder at you with fear, honor, and great reverence/respect.

But because He knows you have lost all confidence in self completely; He is confident that you will not destroy yourself by receiving the praise of men.

God has power; He doesn't permit everybody to use this power at will.

But when you have come to the place of brokenness and have abandoned your all to the Lord, then He will rework you to the place where He can trust and permit you to share and to exercise this power to a certain noticeable measure.

"And Jesus came and spake unto them, saying, All power is given unto me in heaven and in earth. Go ye therefore, and teach all nations, baptizing them in the name of the Father, and of the Son, and of the Holy Ghost" (Matthew 28:18-19)

Studies have shown that the broken have been the ones that have had a share and exercise of this limitless power and authority of Christ all through the history of the Church.

Chapter Nine

The Power Of Brokenness

We cannot fully explain for sure the very power that is in being broken, but one thing is sure there's power in brokenness.

While we are not here to argue about that power, we want to look at Scriptures and characters in the Bible that came to their broken points and the things they accomplished by Grace afterwards.

From the Old Testament to the New, we see men and woman empowered by the Spirit of grace who went about doing feats for the Lord and His kingdom willingly.

Now, I want you to notice one common trend about them, brokenness, willingness, and grace afterwards - which made the difference.

So, the underlying power of brokenness is summed up in one word „GRACE." And the show of it is complete WILLINGNESS and OBEDIENCE.

From the point of being broken, God released grace into

these people's lives that changed their lives forever and that also make them to alter the course of nature and history in their time.

Now, let us examine a few of them.

Some Of God's Broken Heroes

1. Abraham

Beginning with Abraham, let us see the power and effect of brokenness.

Abraham was a grown man already when God called Him to leave His father's land to a land (another) that God will show him and will give him for an inheritance.

God gave him a covenant and promised him a seed that will inherit him and continue with the covenant.

Abraham believed God, step out in obedience to God as much as he knew how to. God honored his faith and credited it with righteousness.

True to God's promise, after Abraham had waited a while - when Abraham was now 100 years old, God gave him the promised son, Isaac through his aged wife Sarah.

Then come one day, when Abraham was beginning to find succor in the child of promise, when Abraham was beginning to have bright hopes for the future, God said to him; Abraham, take your son, the son you love and go to the land of

Moriah and locate a mountain that I will show you and there sacrifice your son for an offering unto me. (Genesis 22: 2)

Before now, Abraham had passed several tests with the Lord and some he had also failed. But for this one, nothing compares to it.

Remember we have said in the previous chapter that brokenness is not necessarily a once and for a time experience; we can and may experience several brokenness until God's course is accomplished in our lives.

Did you think that this was a cheap decision for Abraham to take?

Well, Abraham had come to surrender all His life to God, at this point, Abraham was ready to trust God with all things and in all situations.

He knew that what he has is not his own; his life was no longer his, his sons were not his, his money was not really his, he was a custodian for the great Father-God in His estate.

The Scripture says that Abraham willingly obeyed God and trusted Him completely and was fully persuaded that God was able to raise Isaac from the dead.

"By faith Abraham, when he was tested, offered up Isaac, and he who had received the promises was in the act of offering up his only son, of whom it was said, "Through Isaac shall your offspring be named." He considered that God was able even to raise him from the dead, from which, figuratively speaking, he did receive him back." (Hebrews 11:17-19, ESV)

Such is the power of brokenness.

Abraham did what God asked Him to do in willingly and in complete obedience. The rest is history. Abraham today is known and recognized as the father of faith because through brokenness, he was able to come to a point of complete surrender, trust, dependence and obedience to the will and word of God.

This is where God wants to bring you to. Are you ready for this?

Can you see the power of being broken?

Do you see how beautiful life will become when you learn to give up claim and ownership of your very life, possession, and things?

It frees the life of work, headaches, anxiety, and pain. And then replaces it with ease, freedom, love, beauty, assurance, confidence, and REST.

There's beauty in brokenness my friend.

2. Moses

Moses was God's mightiest prophet in the Old Testament; the „face to face with God" prophet that God used to humble the ancient Egyptian civilization and world power of the day.

But was Moses always that way? The answer is a big NO.

Moses was fearful, chicken hearted, murderer, renegade, hot temper, a stammerer, to name a few.

But what accounted for the change and boldness of Moses afterwards?

It was his several encounters with God that brought about his brokenness.

First, we see Moses born when Pharaoh decreed that all Hebrew male children be killed.

God saved him by having Pharaoh's daughter pick him up by the riverbank adopting him as her very own son.

That was grace at work.

The next time we saw Moses was him coming out to check on his people (he kept that knowledge with him – perhaps his family members kept telling him who he really was at every opportunity they had to talk with him).

Then he met an Egyptian mistreating one of his brethren, he killed the Egyptian and went his way.

The next time he wanted to settle between his brothers, they fooled him by exposing his murder the previous day.

Away, he fled Egypt as a coward when he discovered that Pharaoh now knew what he did.

He started living in Midian where he got married and worked for the chief priest of the city as a shepherd.

Then he met God in the burning and after a series of brokenness, he accepted the call of God for his life even though he still was reluctant.

With confidence that God was with him, that he has no power of his own, he went to Egypt, confronted Pharaoh (the same person that wanted him dead some years before) and with mighty acts brought out the children of Israel from their bondage in Egypt.

Even after all these feats, Moses kept asking God for reassurances every now and then.

"And Moses said unto the LORD, See, thou sayest unto me, Bring up this people: and thou hast not let me know whom thou wilt send with me. Yet thou hast said, I know thee by name, and thou hast also found grace in my sight. Now therefore, I pray thee, if I have found grace in thy sight, shew me now thy way, that I may know thee, that I may find grace in thy sight: and consider that this nation *is* thy people. And he said, My presence shall go *with thee*, and I will give thee rest. And he said unto him, If thy presence go not *with me*, carry us not up hence. For wherein shall it be known here that I and thy people have found grace in thy sight? *is it* not in that thou goest with us? so shall we be separated, I and thy people, from all the people that *are* upon the face of the earth. And the LORD said unto Moses, I will do this thing also that thou hast spoken for thou hast found grace in my sight, and I know thee by name. And he said, I beseech thee, shew me thy glory." (Exodus 33:12-18, KJV)

God was kind to Moses and then gave him what he asked for.

God showed himself to Moses physically. Moses saw the Lord and that was the last assurance that he needed.

This is what brokenness does to you.

If you want to have God's assurance in your life and ministry, you must seek the Lord until you have an experience with His tangible presence,

When you do, you will be quick to forget yourself and to trust completely in His grace and glory. Moses had lost all confidence in self; all He needed was God and God alone.

Where's your confidence, self, or God?

You must be broken to know confidence, dependence and complete reliance on God and God alone.

Have you come to this point in your life? If not, let God break you.

3. Peter

What about Peter the garrulous, talkative, fearful, susceptible, and denier?

Peter was not a confident person; yes, he could talk at anything before thinking through it.

Jesus was always patient with Him, but also knew that Peter had to come to his broken point before he can be fit for the Lord's utmost use.

Peter could not be God's best until he had surrendered his weaknesses to the Lord, swapping it for His grace.

One day, Jesus told his disciples that he was going to be betrayed by one of them into the hands of the Jews who want Him dead and they in turn will turn Him over to the gentiles to be crucified.

Peter spoke up as usual and rebuked the Lord for saying it.

Then at another time, when He discovered that the Lord's will was set and fixed for death, he then claimed that he was going to die with Him.

He (Peter) was a person who was full of himself.

He so believed in his physical ability and powers to get things done.

Self-confidence is not bad but not when it comes to walking with the Lord. You must throw away your self-confidence and power in exchange for God's confidence and grace if you want God's power to be displayed and seen through you.

One way to have this happen in a person is for God to break you.

Fast forward some few weeks after, Jesus was arrested and was being taken in for questioning.

Peter thought he could fight for the Lord (not bad at all – I love his commitment and drive, but was all in the flesh), cut off one of high priest servant's ear.

Then he went on to the place (palace) where the Lord was being tried, mine, when he saw what they were doing to the Lord, he was afraid.

All other disciples had fled, ran away when they saw the soldiers and armed persons that came to arrest the Lord, but stubborn-strong willed Peter followed on because he wanted to see the end.

He had said that he will die with the Lord, so he must stand by what he said.

But when Peter was faced with the real situation, when he saw what was happening, he denied his Lord 3 times even before a girl, a woman. (Luke 22:54-62)

A girl!

Yes, Peter denied Jesus before a girl. Peter's denial of His Lord broke him.

He wept, the Scripture says (Luke 22:62) He saw his utter helplessness and weakness.

He saw his inability and failure of self; he saw how gullible and weak he really was; and then he wept.

That was the turning point for Peter.

In that state, he knew he could by no means of natural pride and arrogance stand for the Lord. He needed something more than self-confidence; he needed the fire of the Holy

Ghost.

He needed grace and courage born of the Spirit of grace.

When Jesus came back from the dead (resurrected), He restored Peter. And at the restoration, Peter will no longer boast in his confidence; all he could say and was even slow to say was: Yes Lord, you know..., Yes Lord, you know... Lord you know everything... (John 21:15-17)

It was a different Peter.

He could not as he used to just blurt out answers based on his estimate of himself.

No, he was careful to answer and answer by pushing it back on the Lord..." Yes Lord, you know..."

This is what you should do with yourself now.

Do not ever come to the Lord with a confident yes in yourself. No, come to Him with a yes in HIM.

Of course, by the time the Holy Ghost fire joined in with Peter's „Yes Lord, You know..., " he was turned into another man.

The same person who denied his Lord before a young girl would defend His Lord before thousands of people —worshippers.

He even defended his Lord leading to his being beaten, imprisoned and eventual murder. That is the power of brokenness at work.

4. Paul

Radical, self, and strong willed, determined to destroy the faith of the Lord Jesus Christ, the young Paul (known as Saul of Tarsus at the time) will not take a no for anything that has to do with Christians.

He not only was going to drive out the Christian faith from Jerusalem, but he was also bent on doing that even to neighboring countries.

He worked at it, got the permission and authorization of the government of his day to do it. But as he went on doing what he felt called to do, he met the Lord.

Meeting the Lord on that hot afternoon day became for Paul the turning point, the most remarkable moment of his life.

That was the day; the blindness was removed from his eyes. It was his aha moment.

At the instance of Paul's meeting with the Lord, a realization came on him. He saw the truth. It broke him of course.

His physical eyes sight was taken away for 3 days so he could see the real thing with the eyes of his spirit.

It was the defining moment for Saul of Tarsus.

He came from that broken point to embrace new thought, fresh Holy Spirit ideas and concepts. And from that experience, he was able to see who the Lord really is, who the Jewish messiah really is.

It was different from what he had spent years to learn and train as a Jewish rabbi.

Yet he knew he had to give up all his learning in the Pharisaic discipline, order, and mannerism.

Giving up all his learning and position as a Pharisee, and then to accept the simple Light and truth that Jesus (the humble Galilean) is the Messiah was life changing for Paul.

You may never fully know how much Paul gave up for the knowledge of Christ. (Philippians 3:1-11)

Yet, he was broken enough to do it.

He could have in his pride and high estate held on like many other Jews to his former teachings and learning as a Pharisee, but he gave them all up for the Light of Life.

And the rest is history – oh the power of God that worked in and through Paul to bless and still blessing the world today.

And best of all, God got glory for His life.

Did you know the many people who are held bound by knowledge and are not able to come to the place where God can use them because of their education?

Please give up your learning, degrees, philosophies that are anti-Christ and embrace the simple truth of the gospel of Christ if you want God to have you and use you for His glory.

You may even have to surrender those seminary and theological teachings that deny the power and glory of Christ today.

Jesus Christ is the same yesterday, today and forever. Do you believe that?

Can you confidently say that?

Until and only until you can say that you have not come to your broken point and God may not be able to use you.

Chapter Ten
Now I Surrender All

What else do we need to tell you that we have not said? The broken point, all of us experience it in life.

It is what you make out of it (your surrender) that eventually matters.

Yet God wants you to come to this point in your life, now. Good for you if you yield to the wooing of the Spirit and then willingly surrender now.

But if you do not and God must have to break you, He will if it is to serve His purpose and glory.

The Signature of Brokenness

To help you get on the path of brokenness, here are 3 things you must learn.

1. Repentance

Repentance is the signature of the broken.

If you learn to repent all the time, God will see you fit for His visitation and holy habitation that will bring about His praise and glory in your life.

So do not be stubborn about change, when you miss it and are convicted by the Spirit or even man, repent.

And be quick to it; be quick to repent like King David. (2 Samuel 12:1-13)

Because David knew how to repent and repent fast, God used him despite all his sins. God even said that David was a man after His own heart. (See 1 Samuel 13:14, Acts 13:22)

Be quick to repent, please.

2. Willingness

Another thing that you must learn if you desire being broken by the Lord for His glory is willingness.

You must be disposed and inclined to God's word, correction, instructions, and discipline. You do not have to be forced by the Lord to respond to His pleadings and biddings.

Please be a willing person.

"If you are willing and obedient, you shall eat the good of the land; but if you refuse and rebel, you shall be eaten by the sword; for the mouth of the LORD has spoken."
(Isaiah 1:19-20, ESV)

3. Obedience

The next step that comes after willingness on the ladder of brokenness is obedience.

To have the Lord break you and get the best out of you, you must be a person who readily obeys the Lord.

Obedience is central to the walk of faith and so must be learned by every of God's greats and pilgrims.

The man who will be broken by God must be one who is disposed to obedience to the word and the Spirit of God 100 percent of the time.

4. Patient

Now, we must not forget to add that patient is a necessary condition for the maturing of your faith and your obedience.

It takes time for some things to grow and become.

It will take a little time for God's hand of glory to begin to show in your life after He has broken you.

"...be not slothful, but followers of them who through faith and patience inherit the promises." (Hebrews 6:12, KJV)

Conclusion

You have read the book and are acquainted with the truth of God's word around brokenness; what's left now is what you do with what you have read.

I want to urge you to allow the Holy Spirit tattooed these truths in your spirit until you begin to walk in the reality of them.

Broken before the Lord, your usefulness in the service of the Lord is unlimited.

Do you want the Lord to bless you and make you a blessing to the world; you've got to learn to be broken.

So, it's time you get to your broken point, and there the Lord will make you again into His choice image in Christ.

All the best!

Made in the USA
Middletown, DE
28 October 2023

41292432R20050